THE GUY WHO WAS FIVE MINUTES LATE

by Bill Grossman

illustrated by Judy Glasser

Harper & Row, Publishers

Library of Congress Cataloging-in-Publication Data
Grossman, Bill.
    The guy who was five minutes late / by Bill Grossman ; illustrated
by Judy Glasser.
        p.   cm.
    Summary: A baby, born five minutes late, grows up being five
minutes behind for everything until he meets his own true love and
discovers he's right on time after all.
    ISBN 0-06-022268-9 : $. — ISBN 0-06-022269-7 (lib. bdg.) :
$
    [1. Time—Fiction.   2. Individuality—Fiction.   3. Stories in
rhyme.]   I. Glasser, Judy, ill.   II. Title.
PZ8.3.G914G4   1990   89-36336
[E]—dc20   CIP
                                                                        AC

10 9 8 7 6 5 4 3 2 1

First Edition

For Mom and Freddie,
and Dearie, and Glumple.
               —B.G.

For ⓉⓂ
  —J.G.

A baby was born
On a lovely spring morn
(I don't remember the date).

"A good-looking boy,"
Said his mother with joy.
"But darn it! He's five minutes late."

Yep, five minutes late.
He'd made them all wait.
And no one at first seemed to mind.

But to people's surprise,
As he grew up in size,
He remained five minutes behind.

By night

or by day,

At work

or at play,

He always was five minutes late.

When boating

or biking

Or sledding

or hiking,

He always made everyone wait.

He watched every show
From the very last row—
Too late to get a good seat.

When his family ate,
He was five minutes late
And wound up with little to eat.

He grew up quite frail

And thin as a rail,

And was late for church and for school.

He always missed trains

And buses and planes,

So he walked everywhere as a rule.

He failed at sports
Of all different sorts.
When he raced, other runners would find him
Alone in last place
At the end of the race,
Having started five minutes behind them.

At twenty he met
A young lady and set
A time for them both to be wed.

He was five minutes late,
And she wouldn't wait,
So she married his brother instead.

He felt a bit sad
Till he read in an ad:
HUSBAND WANTED FOR SWEET PRINCESS CARRIE.
BE AT THE GATE
OF THE PALACE AT EIGHT,
WHERE THE PRINCESS WILL CHOOSE WHO SHE'LL MARRY.

To be able to marry
The sweet Princess Carrie,
He knew that he'd have to look great.

So he ran out to buy
A suit with a tie
To wear to the palace at eight.

When he got to the store,
A sign on the door
Said: WE'RE OUT OF SUITS. YOU'RE TOO LATE.

"Phooey," he said,
And he went home to bed
And slept until just before eight.

Down at the gate
Of the palace at eight
Stood two hundred handsome young guys,

All the same size
With baby-blue eyes
And spiffy new jackets and ties.

The princess was late,
So they all had to wait
To learn who would win and who'd lose.
They all wondered who
Of that good-looking crew
Was the one the princess would choose.

At five after eight,
Five minutes late,
Came our hero in blue jeans—no suit.
And the handsome young guys
With their jackets and ties
And their baby-blue eyes
Hollered, "Scoot!"

He was turning to go
When a voice said, "Hello,"
And asked, "Did you get here at eight?"

"No, Princess," he said.
"I stayed in my bed
And ended up getting here late."

"How late?" said she.
"Two minutes? Or three?"
"No," he said sheepishly. "Five."

"Five minutes!" she said,
Her face turning red.
"Five minutes! My gosh! Sakes alive!"

He looked so forlorn.
"I guess I was born
Too late by five minutes," he said.

Said she, "So was I!
You're my kind of guy."

And they hurried to church to be wed.

"Princess," said he,
"We're on time, you and me.
But folks are in such a big hurry
That whenever they wait
They think that *we're* late,
When really it's *they* who are early."